Bunnies' ABC

Illustrated by
Garth Williams

A Golden Book • New York
Western Publishing Company, Inc., Racine, Wisconsin 53404

I J K L M

Aa

for alligator

Bb

for bear

Cc

for cat

Dd

for deer

E e

for ermine

Ff

for fish

Gg

for giraffe

Hh for horse

Ii

for ibis

Jj

for jaguar

Kk

for kangaroo

Ll for ladybug

Mm for mouse

Nn for nightingale

Oo for ostrich

P p for panda

Qq

for quail

Rr for rooster

Ss

for seal

Tt for turtle

Uu for unicorn

Vv for vulture

Ww for walrus

Xx

for xenurus

Yy

for yak

Zz

THE
END

for zebra

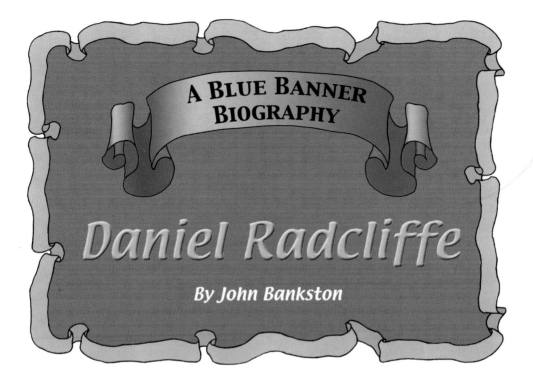

A BLUE BANNER BIOGRAPHY

Daniel Radcliffe

By John Bankston

Mitchell Lane
PUBLISHERS

P.O. Box 196
Hockessin, Delaware 19707
Visit us on the web: www.mitchelllane.com
Comments? email us: mitchelllane@mitchelllane.com

Mitchell Lane
PUBLISHERS

Printing   3   4   5   6   7   8   9

Blue Banner Biographies

Eminem	Sally Field	Jodie Foster
Melissa Gilbert	Rudy Giuliani	Ron Howard
Michael Jackson	Jennifer Lopez	Nelly
Mary-Kate and Ashley Olsen	**Daniel Radcliffe**	Selena
Shirley Temple	Richie Valens	Rita Williams-Garcia

Library of Congress Cataloging-in-Publication Data
Bankston, John, 1974-
      Daniel Radcliffe / John Bankston.
          p. cm. — (A blue banner biography)
  Summary: A biography of the young actor chosen to portray Harry Potter in the "Harry Potter" movies.
  Filmography (p.).
  Includes bibliographical references and index.
     ISBN 1-58415-250-8 (library bound)
  1. Radcliffe, Daniel, 1989—Juvenile literature. 2. Motion picture actors and actresses—Great Britain—Biography—Juvenile literature. [1. Radcliffe, Daniel, 1989- 2. Actors and actresses.] I. Title. II. Series.
PN2598.R27B36 2003
791.43'028'092--dc21

2003000678

ABOUT THE AUTHOR: Born in Boston, Massachussetts, **John Bankston** began publishing articles in newspapers and magazines while still a teenager. Since then, he has written over two hundred articles, and contributed chapters to books such as *Crimes of Passion,* and *Death Row 2000,* which have been sold in bookstores across the world. He has written numerous biographies for young adults, including Mandy Moore and Alexander Fleming and the Story of Penicillin (Mitchell Lane). He currently lives in Portland, Oregon.
PHOTO CREDITS: Cover: Getty Images; p. 4 Scott Barbour/Getty Images; p. 7 Henry McGee/Globe Photos, Inc.; p. 13 Lawrence Lucier/Getty Images; p. 17 Reuters NewMedia Inc./Corbis; p. 18 AP Photo/Shuji Kajiyama; p. 22 AP Photo; p. 29 Warner Bros./Getty Images
ACKNOWLEDGMENTS: The following story has been thoroughly researched, and to the best of our knowledge, represents a true story. While every possible effort has been made to ensure accuracy, the publisher will not assume liability for damages caused by inaccuracies in the data, and makes no warranty on the accuracy of the information contained herein. This story has not been authorized nor endorsed by Daniel Radcliffe.

CONTENTS

Daniel Radcliffe didn't want to be famous. He wanted a career as an actor. Before he was twelve years old, he would have both fame and a career.

Dreams

*D*aniel Radcliffe's quiet tub-time was interrupted by a phone call. It was an important one. It was the call that would change his life.

"I was in the bath when my Dad came in and said they'd called [to tell] me I was Harry Potter," Daniel told the *Christian Science Monitor*. "I was so happy I cried." He later asked his parents if it had all been a dream. It wasn't.

The Harry Potter series has sold millions of books across the world. Not only are they loved by both kids and adults, everyone who read them imagined what Harry Potter would look like, and how he'd act. When the movie was being cast, thousands of young actors tried out for the part. When he earned the role, Daniel faced an enormous amount of pressure along with the grim reality that his happy dream could turn into a nightmare if the public didn't accept him.

At least he had a supportive family—eventually.

But in the beginning, his parents didn't want him to act. That's not surprising. After all, acting careers are unstable and filled with rejection. A professional actor can go years without work, being turned down at every audition — the interview process of getting a job. It's not easy hearing you're "too tall, too short, too old, too young." Few adults pursue acting as a career for very long.

When Daniel Radcliffe told his parents he wanted to be an actor, he was just five years old.

When Daniel told his parents he wanted to be an actor, however, he was five years old. His parents didn't think it was a good idea. Daniel's mom and dad actually knew the world of show business pretty well, unlike most parents who think such a career is a bad choice.

Daniel's father, Alan Radcliffe, was a literary agent with International Creative Management (ICM). The company represents some of the best known writers, actors and film-makers in the world. Because of his job, Daniel's father often came in contact with actors.

Daniel's mother, Marcia Gresham, saw even more performers struggling to get work. Marcia is a casting director. That means she auditions hundreds of professional actors. She selects the lucky few who get to meet with a project's producers and directors, the ones who make the final decision on who gets hired.

Alan and Marcia knew even more about acting's ups and downs because they'd gotten their start working as actors when they were in their twenties. By the time Daniel Alan Radcliffe was born on July 23, 1989 in Lon-

Daniel's mother Marsha and his father Alan didn't want their son to become a professional actor. They'd been actors and they knew how hard it was. What they didn't know was how stubborn their only child could be when it came to pursuing his dream.

don, England, his parents were in their thirties and they knew one thing. Their only child *wasn't* going to be an actor.

Daniel eventually changed their minds.

Growing up in an upper middle class neighborhood where most of the homes are worth over half a million dollars, Daniel had an idyllic childhood. There was often time for playing soccer and other sports with his "mates," or watching professional wrestling and Formula One racing on television. Yet even as he began attending an all-boys private school, he still knew he wanted to act.

> *Daniel's parents were both in their thirties and did not want their only child to be an actor.*

His parents kept putting him off. Because they both knew plenty of directors and producers, either one of them could have gotten Daniel an audition with just a phone call. So for a while Daniel contented himself with school plays.

He told Shep Morgan of *E! Online*, "I think my earliest memory of acting was playing a monkey in a school play, when I was about six. I had floppy ears and orange makeup and I had to wear tights. I think I went on and danced around for about 40 seconds or something. I hope nobody ever digs up a picture of me in that, because it was embarrassing."

But when he learned that the British Broadcasting Corporation (BBC) was casting for the title role of a major miniseries, he begged his mother to send them his photograph. She finally agreed, and not long afterward he got to go on his first audition.

Despite his inexperience, his first professional audition led to his first job. He got the part. It wasn't just his first big break. It was the job which would change his life.

> *Despite Daniel's inexperience, his first professional audition led to his first job. It was the job that would change his life.*

Daniel and David

When English writer Charles Dickens was twelve years old, his father fell on hard times. John Dickens worked for the Royal Navy, but he and his wife spent far more money than his job paid. In the 1820s, people who couldn't afford to pay the debts they owed wound up in places like Marshalsea Prison, where John was jailed.

By today's standards, it was an odd prison. Prisoners could live with their families, and John's wife and children moved in with him. They could come and go as they pleased, but John couldn't leave until the debt was paid off. Since he couldn't work, he was forced to rely on his son. Charles was a talented student, but his family's debt drove him from school and forced him to work in a factory. It was a miserable life. Although it lasted just a few months, Charles' period of poverty and labor left a permanent scar on him.

He never told his wife about that time. He never told his children. Instead he described it in a book. By the time *The Personal History of David Copperfield* was published in 1850, Dickens was in his late thirties, a very successful author with over half a dozen novels to his credit. *David Copperfield* is one of his best loved novels. It is also the most personal and autobiographical.

In 1999, the British Broadcasting Corporation (BBC) began filming *David Copperfield* as a multi-episode program. Daniel would be playing David Copperfield when he was a boy. Although he'd only appear in the first two episodes, his part was very important.

The role, his first as a professional, was also very challenging. Daniel lived in a nice neighborhood with a loving family and two dogs. He went to a private school where the tuition was over $12,000 a year.

Yet his character was a boy who had experienced the worst kinds of poverty and loss. Daniel had to be believable even though his background was completely different. But then that's what acting is all about.

The production also aired in the United States on the Public Broadcasting System's *Masterpiece Theatre*. It co-

Daniel's first role as a professional actor was challenging. The character was a boy who had experienced poverty and loss.

starred two of England's most famous actors, Ian McKellen and Dame Maggie Smith. Daniel had most of his scenes with Bob Hoskins, who played Mr. Micawber. Although Hoskins is a respected theater actor, he's perhaps best known for the 1988 movie, *Who Framed Roger Rabbit?*, in which he co-starred with a cartoon.

Daniel was a bit more lively than a cartoon bunny. As Hoskins recalled in an interview with *People* magazine, Daniel was pretty talented with limericks. "He knows a lot more than I do!" Bob laughed. One of the limericks was a re-worked version of "Mary Had a Little Lamb," which Hoskins joked was "quite rude."

When filming on *David Copperfield* ended, Daniel wanted to keep acting. As he told *The Hollywood Reporter*, he was "not very fond of school" although he liked English and science. Nevertheless, under British law, actors under the age of eighteen can only work four hours a day. They have to attend classes with an on-set tutor for an additional four hours. So in a way, he could go to school and still act.

Under British law, actors under the age of eighteen can only work four hours a day, and must attend classes with a tutor.

His parents agreed to let him audition for other parts. He was quickly cast in *The Tailor of Panama* as one of the Tailor's sons. The part allowed him to work with top-notch actors like Geoffrey Rush and Pierce Brosnan, who is best-known for his "James Bond" roles.

He probably grew closest to Jamie Lee Curtis, who played the role of his mother. An actress who got her start in horror movies, Curtis has also written several children's books and has kids of her own. Curtis had

Although Daniel had read a couple of the books, he wasn't the biggest Harry Potter fan in the world. Still, several very important people took one look at Daniel and knew he should play the part.

read several books by a one-time unemployed single mom whose stories about the Hogwarts School of Witchcraft and Wizardy were huge bestsellers. She recalled for *Entertainment Weekly*, "The first time I laid eyes on this kid (Daniel), I said, 'He's Harry Potter. He should be Harry Potter.' He's the perfect choice."

Daniel Radcliffe wasn't exactly the biggest Harry Potter fan in his class. "My best friend at school, Alex Berman, is a fanatic about Harry Potter," Daniel explained to the *Christian Science Monitor*. "I believe he'd read the fourth book six or eight times, which is pretty impressive."

> *It was pretty much impossible to be ten years old and not know who Harry Potter was.*

But it was pretty much impossible to be ten years old and not know who Harry Potter was. Daniel had read a couple of the books so he was familiar with the story. But he never thought he'd be in the movie. Yet even as he was going about his daily life, a director he'd never met already realized the ten-year-old lad was just the actor he wanted.

CHAPTER 3

The Trouble with Casting Harry

*I*n the early 1990s, Joanne Rowling (ROLL-ing) was a struggling single mother with a dream. Recently divorced and without a job, she found herself mulling over a story that had come to her a few years before. She'd been stuck on a train, and had imagined a story about a very special young man.

In 1993, she started writing the story down. Sometimes scribbling on scraps of paper at a nearby coffee shop, she wrote the book as she occasionally rocked her baby Jessica with her free hand. When she finished, she sent it to an agent she picked out of a book because she liked his name—Christopher Little. He liked it enough to represent her. Even then it took over a year and several rejections before the book found a publisher.

There was a slight problem. The publisher told Joanne that boys were less likely to buy a book written by a woman.

The solution was simple. Joanne took the initials of her first name and Kathleen, her middle name. The rest is publishing history. The story of *Harry Potter and the Philosopher's Stone* by J.K. Rowling was an immediate hit when it was published in the United Kingdom in 1997. She received more than $100,000 for the U.S. rights, a huge amount for a children's book by a first-time author. Slightly retitled as *Harry Potter and the Sorcerer's Stone*, the book appeared in the United States in 1998 and hit the best-seller lists right away.

Rowling has said that she always pictured the Harry Potter stories as a seven-book series. As of the summer of 2003 she had completed four more. The Harry Potter books have sold over 200 million copies.

In the year 2000 they were about to become a movie. Warner Brothers Pictures bought the rights to make a movie of the books. They hired Chris Columbus, who'd directed the *Home Alone* series, to direct the first two Harry Potter films. Columbus and Rowling both wanted a British actor for the part. A casting call went out in April for boys aged nine to eleven to play Harry. The response was overwhelming. According to the English newspaper *Manchester Guardian*, a reported 60,000 boys

In the year 2000, the first Harry Potter book was about to become a movie. The director wanted a British actor to play Harry.

When J.K. Rowling (center) was a struggling single mother she'd written the first Harry Potter book and based the part of Hermione on herself. The books made her rich and the parts of Hermione and Harry made Emma Watson (right) and Daniel Radcliffe (left) famous.

tried out for the part—meeting the casting director, reading parts of the scripts, being videotaped. None of them was right.

By August, Columbus was growing more and more upset. He'd spent several months and at least one million dollars of Warner Brothers' money trying to find the right boy to play Harry Potter.

"These are magical roles, the kind that come around once in a lifetime," Warner Brothers President Lorenzo di Bonaventura told *Scholastic News Service*. "They required talented children who can bring magic to the screen."

Part of being a movie star is promoting a film – doing interviews, attending premieres, and flying all over the world. Here Daniel Radcliffe promotes the movie Harry Potter and the Chamber of Secrets *in Tokyo, Japan.*

Part of Columbus's problem came because he believed he knew the child who had that magic.

"Our casting director left the picture," he admitted to *The Hollywood Reporter*, "because she was getting so frustrated. At one point she turned on me because I had rejected everyone. She said, 'Who do you want?!' I picked up a copy of the video for *David Copperfield* that had Daniel Radcliffe on the cover and said, 'This is who I want.'"

There was only one problem. Daniel's parents had already been asked if their son could play the part. They refused. They both realized the Harry Potter movies would be huge. Whoever starred in them would become instantly famous, recognized in the United States and England and just about everywhere else that there are movie theaters. That type of fame would be tough enough for an adult to deal with. For a kid it could forever change his life, and not necessarily for the better.

Daniel would stop being "Daniel Radcliffe, actor," and become Harry Potter. Alan and Marcia were afraid he'd lose his childhood, or worse. The many stories about child stars who grow up to be troubled adults are legendary.

"They wouldn't even meet with us," Columbus confessed to the *Hollywood Reporter*. The director reached a standstill. He didn't want the actors who were available. The actor he did want wasn't available.

And then everything changed. It didn't change because of a movie, it changed because of a play. A play Daniel wasn't even in.

> *Daniel's parents refused to allow him to play the part of Harry Potter. They wouldn't even meet with the director.*

As Big as a
Beatle

"I went to see the play *Stones in His Pockets* with my mom and dad," Daniel told the *Christian Science Monitor*. "In the row in front of us were two men who knew my dad."

One was screenwriter Steven Kloves, whose credits included the movie *Wonder Boys,* starring Tobey Maguire. The other was producer David Heyman. Heyman was currently producing *Harry Potter and the Sorcerer's Stone*. Kloves had written the movie's screenplay. It must have been fate, the two of them sitting just one row from the young man their director wanted to play Harry Potter.

Heyman was acquainted with Daniel's father Alan. During the play's intermission, Alan spoke with the two men. When the conversation was over, he turned to his son.

"I didn't know who they were," Daniel admitted to the *Monitor*, "but my Dad asked if I'd like to go to the studio and have lunch with them."

Daniel's "lunch at the studio" turned into a full-fledged audition, including videotaped performances called screen tests. Tested on his own twice, he was also paired with his future co-stars: Emma Watson who would play the bright and skillful Hermione and Rupert Grint, who'd play Ron, the klutzy and comic spell-caster.

"Even though I have been to auditions before… this is such a big thing, and the books are so successful," Daniel told *The Hollywood Reporter*. "It was really scary."

He needn't have worried. Director Columbus remembers the screen test with Daniel, Emma and Rupert. "We didn't want to cast any of the children until we'd found Harry," Columbus told the *Hollywood Reporter*. "And then we saw the three of them together, we knew this was our trio."

He also knew that his original judgment about Daniel had been correct.

"Daniel is just amazing," Columbus told writer Alona Wartofsky. "He embodies that haunted quality that Harry has. I don't know where he gets it from, be-

> *Daniel was invited to have lunch with the producer and screenwriter of the Harry Potter movie.*

Director Christopher Columbus (right) couldn't believe how perfect Daniel was for the part of Harry Potter. Despite two supportive parents, Daniel managed to play a boy who was troubled and suffering.

cause he has two very stable parents. But this kid has a depth beyond his years."

Daniel's initial enthusiasm for the movie never wore off completely. It was impossible not to walk around the enormous sets, made up to look like The Hogwarts School of Witchcraft and Wizardry, the Dursleys' house where Harry was kept almost a prisoner, and numerous other places once described in Rowling's words and not feel excitement. Daniel was Harry Potter, the star of a one-hundred-million dollar movie. He was reportedly paid slightly more than $100,000. He also knew if the movie tanked, he'd get blamed.

Despite all of the responsibility resting on Daniel's thin shoulders, he never took things too seriously. Robbie Coltrane, who played the gigantic groundskeeper Rubeus Hagrid, bore the brunt of Daniel's pranks. Besides placing a frog in Coltrane's shoe, Daniel also figured out how to re-program the translation system of Coltrane's hi-tech cell phone. By the time Daniel finished with the device, Coltrane's voice messages were all playing back in Turkish.

When Daniel began the first Harry Potter movie, he had already performed in movies, but his two costars had only done school plays.

Daniel had a couple of movies under his belt when he walked on the Harry Potter set, but his co-stars, Rupert and Emma had only done school plays. In the beginning making the movie was an education.

"When you are working with kids like that, you're basically teaching them how to deal with performing in front of the camera. In a school play, you tend to over-act; on film you need to play things down," Columbus explained to *The Hollywood Reporter*. "Once they got into that mind set, which took about two weeks, the shoot went very comfortably. It was just a matter of them finding the reality of any scene.

And it helped that they all got along amazingly well. They never threw tantrums. They were great."

Besides, even as the star of a major motion picture, Daniel's workday was more relaxed than it would have been in the United States. While the laws for child actors are fairly strict in the U.S., they are even more rigid in Britain. In the U.S., director Columbus figured he could have finished shooting Harry Potter in around eighty days. It Britain it took over one hundred because of the law that limits child actors to four hours of work a day. In addition, they have to take a fifteen-minute break each hour. It didn't allow for much time in front of the camera. However, the filmmakers made the most of it, by editing — putting the scenes of film together — while the movie was still being made. This made the post-production period, the time after a movie when the editing, sound effects, music and other elements are added, far shorter.

> **The movie took over one hundred days to complete, due to Britain's strict laws for child actors.**

On November 4, 2001, *Harry Potter and the Sorcerer's Stone* premiered at the Odeon Leicester Square Theatre in London. Over 10,000 fans waited in the chilly night for a glimpse of author J.K. Rowling, musician Sting and movie stars like Ben Stiller. Actor John Hurt asked *Daily Variety*, "Have you seen anything like it? I don't think I've seen Leicester Square so electrified since the Beatles."

And no one felt the electricity more than Daniel. "My face and stomach are vibrating," he told *People* magazine. He'd barely slept the night before, and as he looked out at the hordes of fans, many calling him "Harry" instead of "Daniel," the young actor must have been a bit worried. After all, there was no way to know if the movie would be successful or if the legions of fans would be disappointed by his portrayal. He was the one playing the character millions of kids around the world had already seen in their imaginations. Readers are often disappointed when their favorite books are turned into movies. Sometimes this unhappiness keeps viewers away.

Daniel was playing the character millions of kids around the world had already seen in their imaginations.

The Future's Bright

*T*he funny part is that many reviewers criticized the first Harry Potter movie for being too much like the book. But fans ignored the critics. *Harry Potter and the Sorcerer's Stone* went on to be the second highest grossing movie of all time. Only 1997's *Titanic* earned more money at the box office. Even before it went to DVD and video, Harry Potter made nearly one billion dollars worldwide.

It also changed the lives of Daniel Radcliffe, Emma Watson and Rupert Grint forever. They would have their own Web sites and they'd be pictured on magazine covers. They'd appear on programs they called "chat shows" like David Letterman, Oprah Winfrey and Jay Leno.

There would also be a fair amount of weirdness. Daniel Radcliffe was on the popular MTV program *Total Request Live*. At one point, show host Carson Daly told him to look out on the crowd of teenage girls packed into Times Square.

"There was a girl in a Harry Potter towel and nothing else. It was November in New York," he laughed in an interview with London's *Daily Record* newspaper. "She was out there for ninety minutes holding a sign that said, 'Nothing comes between me and Harry Potter.'"

Emma Watson put it all in perspective, telling an *Associated Press* reporter, "Even when you take away all the glamour, and attention and premieres and everything, it still comes down to the fact that you're acting."

There wasn't really much time for Daniel and his other young castmates to be overwhelmed by the attention. The same month that *Sorcerer's Stone* premiered, the three were back at work on the sequel, *Harry Potter and the Chamber of Secrets.*

It had only been a year and a half since Harry was cast in the movie. By then much had changed. In a way he was more

By the time they began work on the sequel, the three Harry Potter stars were more comfortable in front of the camera.

serious on the set of the sequel, less inclined to play pranks. The three were more comfortable in front of the camera. And the movie was growing up with the stars. The action in *Chamber of Secrets* takes place one year after Harry's discovery that he is a wizard.

In the first film, like the first book, audiences had been introduced to Harry Potter, his slow discovery of his own magical powers and his start at the Hogwarts School. Because his life with the Dursleys had been so unhappy, *Sorcerer's Stone* was about finding a family with Ron and Hermione, and feeling comfortable at his new Hogwarts home.

In *Harry Potter and the Chamber of Secrets*, Daniel had to act with someone who wasn't even there.

Now that family and home were in danger. Just as Harry had gotten a little bit older, *Chamber of Secrets* was aimed at a slightly older audience. While the first movie was mainly funny, the second was a much scarier and darker film with both a giant snake *and* a giant spider. *Chamber of Secrets* also required Daniel's acting abilities to grow as well.

In fact, Daniel had to act with someone who wasn't even there. Dobby, an elf who appears in the movie, was created by a computer. During filming of the scenes with Dobby, filmmakers used an orange ball so Daniel would know where to look. But as he joked to the BBC, "It was kind of hard knowing what kind of facial expression an orange ball is making."

Daniel also needed to speak the Parsel tongue so he could communicate with snakes, hang out of a car suspended thirty feet in the air and do a number of other stunts. He even got to battle a twenty-five foot mechanical snake.

Still, while the filming was difficult, the movie's 2002 opening was a bit easier. The cast had relaxed into their roles. Emma, Rupert and Daniel were all better known but told reporters, they still felt "normal." By then Daniel's father had left his job to manage his son's career and serve as chaperone to movie premieres and interviews.

As Daniel told the *Daily Record* newspaper, "The most important thing for me is to live in the moment doing the best job I can playing Harry and enjoying myself."

Daniel began filming the next Harry Potter movie, *Harry Potter and the Prisoner of Azkaban*, in the spring of 2003. After that, anything is possible.

When Daniel Radcliffe, Rupert Grint and Emma Watson got together, the director knew he'd found his team.

CHRONOLOGY

1989	born on July 23 in London, England
1994	announces to his parents that he wants to be an actor
1999	earns title role in BBC's *David Copperfield*; acts in movie *The Tailor of Panama*
2000	lands role as Harry Potter
2002	wins Best Newcomer Award at Variety Club
2003	begins production of *Harry Potter and the Prisoner of Azkaban*

FILMOGRAPHY

1999	*David Copperfield* (TV episodes 1, 2)
2001	*The Tailor of Panama*
2001	*Harry Potter and the Sorcerer's Stone*
2002	*Harry Potter and the Chamber of Secrets*
2004	*Harry Potter and the Prisoner of Azkaban*

FOR FURTHER READING

Books and Magazines:

Churchill, Bonnie. "Welcome to Daniel Radcliffe's World." *Christian Science Monitor*, Nov. 16, 2001, p.17.

Fierman, Daniel. "Casting a Spell." *Entertainment Weekly*, Sept. 1, 2000, p.16.

Gaines, Ann. *J. K. Rowling*. Bear, DE: Mitchell Lane Publishers, 2002.

"Leapin' Wizards." *People,* Nov. 19, 2001, p. 64.

Pulig, Claudia. "Harry To Offer Peek Inside Chamber." *USA Today*, Jun. 10, 2002.

Robey, Tim. "London Greets Harry." *Daily Variety*, Nov. 6, 2001, p. 31.

Rowling, J.K. *Harry Potter and the Chamber of Secrets*. New York: Scholastic Trade, 1999.

Rowling, J.K. *Harry Potter and the Goblet of Fire*. New York: Scholastic Trade, 2000.

Rowling, J.K. *Harry Potter and the Order of the Phoenix*. New York: Scholastic Trade, 2003.

Rowling, J.K. *Harry Potter and the Prisoner of Azkaban*. New York: Scholastic Trade, 1999.

Rowling, J.K. *Harry Potter and the Sorcerer's Stone*. New York: Scholastic Trade, 1998.

Spelling, Ian. "Harry." Oregonian (Knight/Ridder), Dec. 29, 2002.

On the Web:

Daniel Radcliffe Q&A
http://www.eonline.com/Features/Features/HarryPotter/Qa

David Copperfield
http://www.pbs.org/wgbh/masterpiece/archive/programs/
davidcopperfield/ei_radcliffe.html

Harry Potter
http://harrypotter.warnerbros.com

J. K. Rowing
http://www.edupaperback.org/authorbios/Rowling_JK.html

INDEX